P9-AGW-278

A Note to Parents and Caregivers:

With a focus on math, science, and social studies, *Read-it!* Readers support both the learning of content information and the extension of more complex reading skills. They encourage the development of problem-solving skills that help children expand their thinking.

 The PURPLE LEVEL presents basic topics and objects using high frequency words and simple language patterns.

 The RED LEVEL presents familiar topics using common words and repeating sentence patterns.

 The BLUE LEVEL presents new ideas using a larger vocabulary and varied sentence structure.

 The YELLOW LEVEL presents more challenging ideas, a broad vocabulary, and wide variety in sentence structure.

 The GREEN LEVEL presents more complex ideas, an extended vocabulary range, and expanded language structures.

 The ORANGE LEVEL presents a wide range of ideas and concepts using challenging vocabulary and complex language structures.

When sharing a content focused book with your child, read to find out facts and concepts, pausing often to restate and talk about the new information. The realistic story format provides an opportunity to talk about the language used, and to learn about reading to problem-solve for information. Encourage children to measure, make maps, and consider other situations that allow them to apply what they are learning.

There is no right or wrong way to share books with children. Find time to read and share new learning with your child, and pass on the legacy of literacy.

Adria F. Klein, Ph.D.
Professor Emeritus
California State University
San Bernardino, California

Editor: Julie Gassman
Designer: Hilary Wacholz
Art Director: Heather Kindseth
Managing Editor: Christianne Jones
The illustrations in this book were created with acrylics, colored pencil,
and digital media.

Picture Window Books
151 Good Counsel Drive
P.O. Box 669
Mankato, MN 56002-0669
877-845-8392
www.picturewindowbooks.com

Printed in the United States of America.

All books published by Picture Window Books
are manufactured with paper containing at least
10 percent post-consumer waste.

Library of Congress Cataloging-in-Publication Data
Blackaby, Susan.
Jenna and the three R's/by Susan Blackaby; illustrated by Sharon Lane Holm.
p. cm. — (Read-it! readers. Science)
Includes bibliographical references.
ISBN 978-1-4048-5257-0
1. Recycling (Waste)—Fiction.] I. Holm, Sharon Lane, ill. II. Title.
PZ7.B5318Jef 2009
[E]—dc22
2008032451

Jenna and the Three R's

by Susan Blackaby
illustrated by Sharon Lane Holm

Special thanks to our advisers for their expertise:

Wei Lin, Ph.D.
Director, Environmental and Conservation Sciences Graduate Program
North Dakota State University

Adria F. Klein, Ph.D.
Professor Emeritus, California State University
San Bernardino, California

PiCTURE WiNDOW BOOKS
Minneapolis, Minnesota

On Saturdays, Jenna and her three older brothers did chores.

Ray took out the trash.

Rick cleaned up the yard.

Rob shopped.

Ray zoomed from room to room. He dumped things into the trash. He dumped newspapers and magazines. He dumped jars and bottles. He carried the trash out to the garbage can.

"Stop!" Jenna yelled.

"You can't dump all this stuff," said Jenna. "Don't you know about the three R's? Reduce, reuse, and recycle. We can recycle most of this stuff."

"Paper, plastic, glass, and tin all go in the recycling bin," she rhymed.

Jenna helped Ray sort the trash and fill the bins.

"Did you know that they make running tracks and sport courts out of old athletic shoes?" said Jenna.

"Really?" said Ray.

"It's true," said Jenna. "All of this stuff can get shredded or crushed or melted. Then it is made into something new."

Rick zipped around the yard. He raked leaves up into a pile.

He started to dump them into the trash can.

"Stop!" Jenna yelled.

"Don't dump all this stuff," said Jenna. "Don't you know about the three R's? Reduce, reuse, and recycle. We can make compost from the leaves. Then if we add compost to soil, it will help new plants grow."

"Green waste can be used again. Put it in the compost bin," she rhymed.

Jenna helped Rick put the leaves in the compost bin.

Rick got ready to mow the lawn.

"Use the push mower," Jenna said. "You can save fuel and get a good workout at the same time. It's good for you."

Rick mowed the lawn. Jenna helped put the grass clippings in the compost bin.

"This bucket is shot," said Rick, pointing at the hole in the bottom. He started to toss the bucket into the trash can.

"Wait!" said Jenna. "We can repot Mom's roses in that bucket. We'll save the roses and reuse the bucket, too."

"Find a new and different way to use the stuff you throw away," she rhymed.

Rob hopped up to go shopping. He had the list, the money, and his car key. He headed for the van parked in the driveway.

"Stop!" Jenna yelled.

"Your carbon footprint is size 200," said Jenna. "You are using too much energy to do your job."

Rob looked at his feet. "What do you mean?" he said.

"Carbon footprints measure the damage we do to nature. The more energy you use, the more damage you do," Jenna said.

"Treat our planet Earth with care. Reduce your impact everywhere," she rhymed.

"I need to reduce my impact?" asked Rob.

"Right," said Jenna. "There are easy ways to make your carbon footprint smaller. For starters, here's your bike helmet."

"Why do I need that?" asked Rob.

"We can ride our bikes to the farmers' market," said Jenna. "If you leave the car at home and buy local food, you will use less gas. That will make our footprint smaller."

"We can use our own bags. We will reduce our garbage by not using plastic bags," Jenna said.

"Reduce! That's one of the three R's," said Rob.

Jenna grinned.

Rob and Jenna rode their bikes to the
farmers' market.

By the time Jenna and Rob got home, everyone was hungry. Ray chopped the tomatoes.

Rick chopped the peppers.

Rob chopped the mushrooms, and Jenna helped.

Ray started to slide the pizza into the oven. "Stop!" Rick yelled.

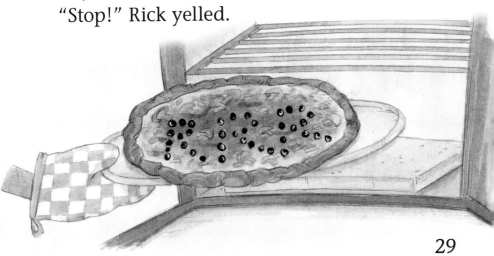

29

"The Three R's are great," said Rick. "But we wouldn't be anywhere without J," said Rob. Jenna smiled.

A Carbon Footprint Activity

What you need:
- Gray construction paper
- A pen or marker to write with
- Scissors

What to do:
1. Draw a large footprint out of the construction paper. Cut it out.
2. On one side, list ways you use the Earth's resources, including transportation, heat, electricity, buying goods shipped to stores from far away, and so on.
3. On the other side of the footprint, list ways you can use the three R's to make your footprint smaller, including carpooling, biking, walking, turning off switches, putting on a sweater, buying local goods, and so on.

Glossary

carbon footprint—the amount of greenhouse gas produced by doing day-to-day activities. A carbon footprint measures how big of an impact you make. The more energy you use, the more damage you do, the bigger your carbon footprint.

compost—living material that has decayed; used to enrich soil

impact—effect or influence of one person or action

recycle—turn waste into resources

reduce—make smaller or less

reuse—use again and again or put to a new use

To Learn More

More Books to Read

Koontz, Robin. *Composting: Nature's Recyclers*. Minneapolis:
    Picture Window Books, 2007.
Green, Jen. *Why Should I Save Energy?* Hauppauge, N.Y.:
    Barron's, 2005.
Hewitt, Sally. *Waste and Recycling*. New York: Crabtree, 2008.

On the Web

FactHound offers a safe, fun way to find Web sites related to
topics in this book. All of the sites on FactHound have been
researched by our staff.

1. Visit *www.facthound.com*
2. Type in this special code: 1404852573
3. Click on the FETCH IT button.

Your trusty FactHound will fetch the best sites for you!

Look for more books in the *Read-it!* Readers: Science series:

Friends and Flowers (life science: bulbs)
The Grass Patch Project (life science: grass)
The Sunflower Farmer (life science: sunflowers)
Surprising Beans (life science: beans)

The Moving Carnival (physical science: motion)
A Secret Matter (physical science: matter)
A Stormy Surprise (physical science: electricity)
Up, Up in the Air (physical science: air)

The Autumn Leaf (Earth science: seasons)
The Busy Spring (Earth science: seasons)
The Cold Winter Day (Earth science: seasons)
The Summer Playground (Earth science: seasons)
Water Wise (Earth science: water conservation)

32